T0132011

Print information available on the last page

Rev. date: 06/06/2019

To order additional copies of this book, contact:
Xlibris
1-888-795-4274
www.Xlibris.com
Orders@Xlibris.com

POZEER. A Dragon that could be the strongest throughout the land.

KADE. A reptile that has the power to control the elemets of TAKYA.

 QYONO-VAL-nest. A god that created TAKYA, the universe and all living beings.

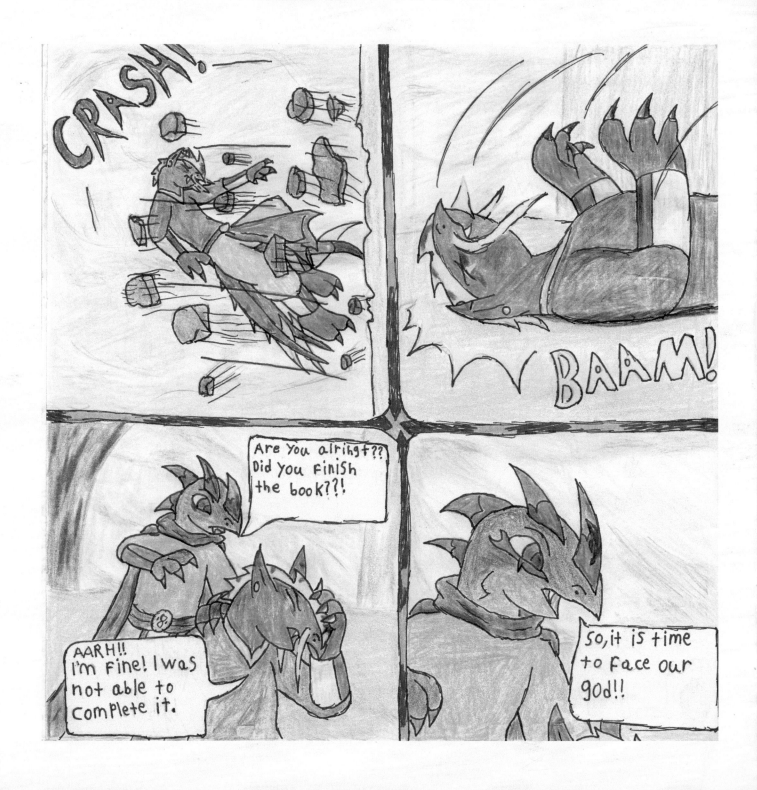

Printed in the United States
By Bookmasters